KU-761-174

MIDNIGHT at THE ZOO

C016254651

A TEMPLAR BOOK

First published in the UK in 2016 by Templar Publishing,
part of the Bonnier Publishing Group,
The Plaza, 535 King's Road, London, SW10 0SZ
www.templarco.co.uk
www.bonnierpublishing.com

Copyright © 2016 by Faye Hanson

1 3 5 7 9 10 8 6 4 2

All rights reserved

ISBN 978-1-78370-327-2 (hardback)
ISBN 978-1-78370-328-9 (paperback)

This book was typeset in Adobe Garamond Pro, Gill Sans and Adobe Caslon
The illustrations were created with pencil and coloured digitally

Designed by Genevieve Webster
Edited by Katie Haworth

Printed in China

To Catherine
and Mikey

Faye Hanson

MIDNIGHT at THE

templar publishing

This is Max and Mia, and today is a VERY special day.

They trundle like elephants into the car.

And cling like monkeys as Mum says goodbye.

They nibble like lemurs on some (early) packed lunch.

And hide at the back like scaredy meerkats.

Then they all scamper off around the zoo.
Everyone is so excited!

They have come to see:

lemurs,

flamingos,

red pandas,

and salamanders.

But not the flick of a tail or swish of a whisker can be seen.

It is very disappointing.

There are no lions.

And not one meerkat . . .

. . . or even a single monkey.

Although Max and Mia do
find some traces of animal life.

It starts to get late . . .

. . . and finally it's time to leave.

For everyone, that is, except Max and Mia,
who suddenly realise they have been . . .

Luckily, Max is very good at being prepared.

Although sometimes Mia has to help him.

And just as the clock strikes midnight . . .

. . . they make a new friend.

They see flouncing flamingos
and fabulous fountains . . .

. . . and mischievous monkeys
in marvellous mountains.

Loud, laughing lemurs
with lanterns alight . . .

... and pandas who prance through
pagodas all night.

They see kingly cats in
their comfortable keep . . .

. . . and as the sun rises they fall fast asleep.

They wake up in the daytime zoo.

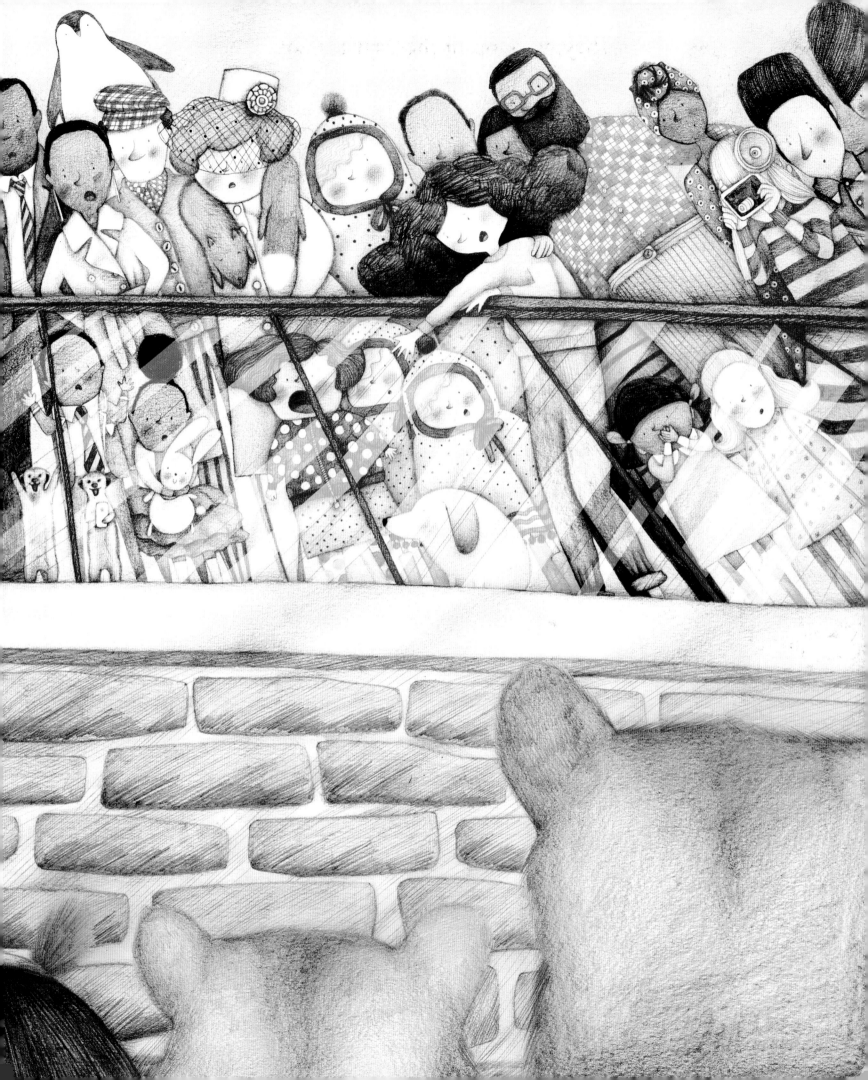

Mum rushes to meet them.
She hugs them tight and they tell her
everything – all about the flouncing flamingos and
prancing pandas and mischievous monkeys!

She doesn't believe them, of course.
But we know it's true.

Also from Faye Hanson:

"For the daydreamers, the storytellers and the creators, *The Wonder* is a
book full of fantasy that explores the joy and the power of the imagination."

— The illustrated forest
www.theillustratedforest.com

ISBN: 978-1-78370-074-5 (hardback)
978-1-78370-114-8 (paperback)